Y0-BQS-234

Two elephants are outside performing their tricks for a lively audience. While blowing toy trumpets with their long trunks, the elephants walk along large wooden logs.

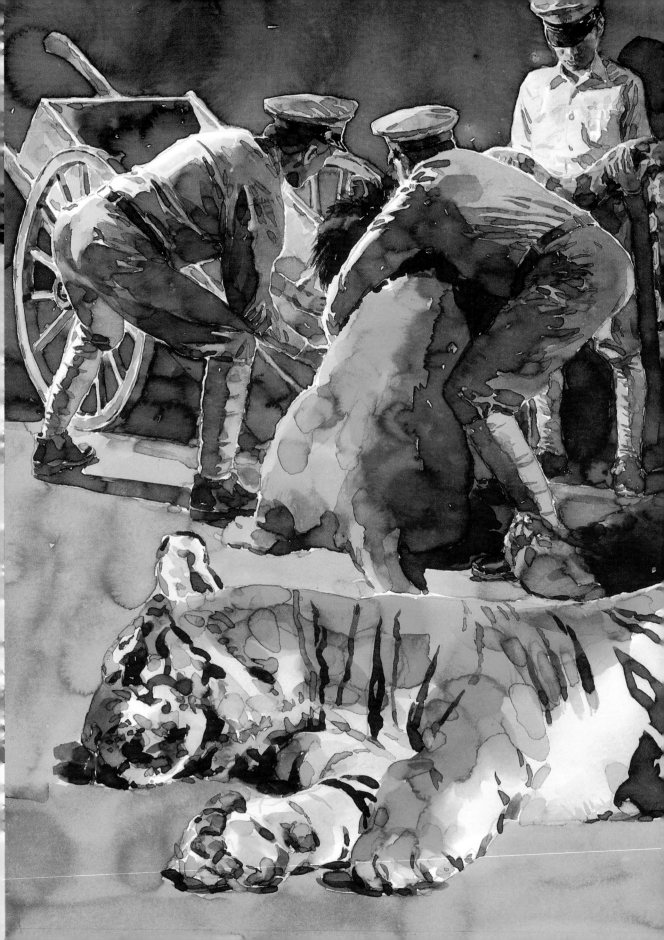

"What would happen if bombs hit the zoo? If the cages were broken and dangerous animals escaped to run wild through the city, it would be terrible! Therefore, by command of the Army, all of the lions, tigers, leopards, bears, and big snakes were poisoned to death.

"By and by, it came time for the three elephants to be killed. They began with John. John loved potatoes, so the elephant keepers mixed poisoned potatoes with the good ones when it was time to feed him. John, however, was a very clever elephant. He ate the good potatoes, but each time he brought a poisoned potato to his mouth with his trunk, he threw it to the ground, *kerplunk!*

" 'As it seems there is no other way,' the zoo keepers said, 'we must inject poison directly into his body.'

"A large syringe, the kind used to give shots to horses, was prepared. But John's skin was so tough that the big needles broke off with a loud *snap,* one after the other. When this did not work, the keepers reluctantly decided to starve him to death. Poor John died seventeen days later.

"Then it was Tonky's and Wanly's turns to die. These two had always gazed at people with loving eyes. They were sweet and gentle-hearted. The zoo keepers wanted so much to keep Tonky and Wanly alive that they thought of sending them to the zoo in Sendai, far north of Tokyo.

"But what if bombs fell on Sendai? What if the elephants got loose and ran wild there? What would happen then?

"Tonky and Wanly, too, were doomed to be killed at the Ueno Zoo, just like all the other animals.

"The elephant keepers stopped feeding Tonky and Wanly. As the days passed, the elephants became thinner and thinner, weaker and weaker. Whenever a keeper walked by their cage, they would stand up, tottering, as if to beg, 'Give us something to eat. Please, give us water!' Their small, loving eyes began to look like round rubber balls in their drooping, shrunken faces. Their ears seemed too large for their bodies. The once big, strong elephants had become a sad shape.

"All this while, the elephants' trainer loved them as if they were his own children. He could only pace in front of the cage and moan, 'You poor, poor, pitiful elephants!' One day, Tonky and Wanly lifted their heavy bodies, staggered to their feet, and came close to their trainer. Squeezing out what little strength they had left, Tonky and Wanly made their appeal. They stood on their hind legs and lifted their front legs up as high as they could. Then, raising their trunks high in the air, they did their banzai trick. Surely their friend would reward them with food and water as he used to do.

"The trainer could stand it no longer. 'Oh, Tonky! Oh, Wanly!' he wailed, and dashed to the food shed. He carried food and pails of water to them and threw it at their feet. 'Here!' he said, sobbing, and clung to their thin legs. 'Eat your food! Please drink. Drink your water!'

"All of the other keepers pretended not to see what the trainer had done. No one said a word. The director of the zoo just sat very still, biting his lip and gazing at the top of his desk. No one was supposed to give the elephants any food. No one was supposed to give them any water. But everyone was hoping and praying that if the elephants could survive only one more day, the war might be over and the elephants would be saved.

"At last, Tonky and Wanly could no longer move. They just lay on their sides, hardly able to see the white clouds floating in the sky over the zoo. However, their eyes appeared clearer and more beautiful than ever.

"Seeing his beloved elephants dying this way, the elephant trainer felt as if his heart would break. He had no more courage to see them. All of the other keepers felt the same, and they too stayed away from the elephants' cage.

"Over two weeks later, Tonky and Wanly were dead. Both died leaning against the bars of their cage with their trunks stretched high in the air, still trying to do their banzai trick for the people who once fed them.

" 'The elephants are dead! They're dead!' screamed the elephant trainer as he ran into the office. He buried his head in his arms and cried, beating the desk top with his fist.

"The rest of the zoo keepers ran to the elephants' cage and stumbled in. They took hold of Tonky's and Wanly's thin bodies, as if to shake them back to life. Everyone burst into tears, then stroked the elephants' legs and trunks in sorrow.

"Above them, in the bright blue sky, the angry roar of enemy planes returned. Bombs began to drop on Tokyo once more. Still clinging to the elephants, the zoo keepers raised their fists to the sky and implored, 'Stop the war! Stop the war! Stop all wars!'

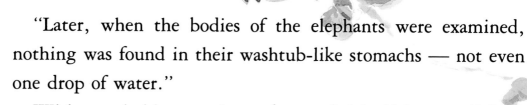

"Later, when the bodies of the elephants were examined, nothing was found in their washtub-like stomachs — not even one drop of water."

With tears in his eyes, the zoo keeper finished his story. "These three elephants — John, Tonky, and Wanly — are now resting peacefully under this monument."

He was still patting the tombstone tenderly as the cherry blossoms fell on the grave, like snowflakes.